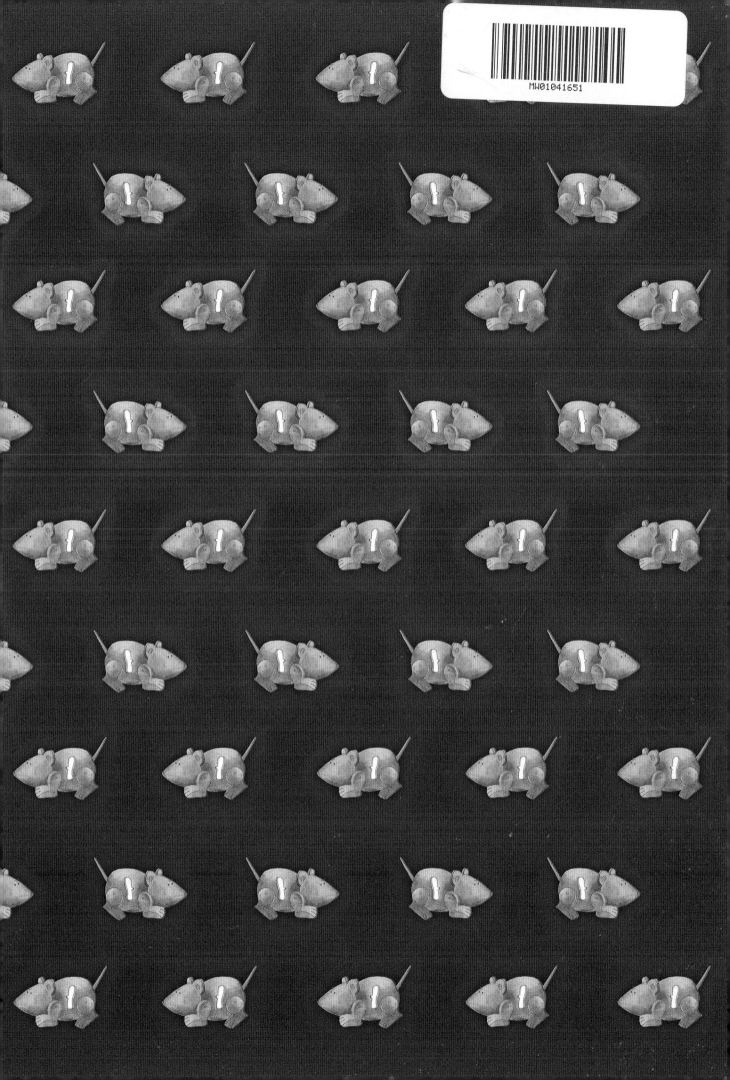

# The WINDUP MOUSE

Written by

## Cao Wenxuan

Illustrated by

## Li Zhang

CARDINAL
MEDIA

Sputter the windup
mouse belonged to
a boy named Jasper.

When Jasper turned her key three times,
Sputter would walk on her own. Click-clack
click-clack click-clack.

Jasper brought Sputter to school each day. At recess he raced her against the other windup toys.

Each day, someone challenged Jasper to a race.
"I'll beat your mouse this time!"

But they never beat Sputter. No one could explain it, but she would always zip a little quicker and zoom a little farther...

...when Jasper cheered for her.

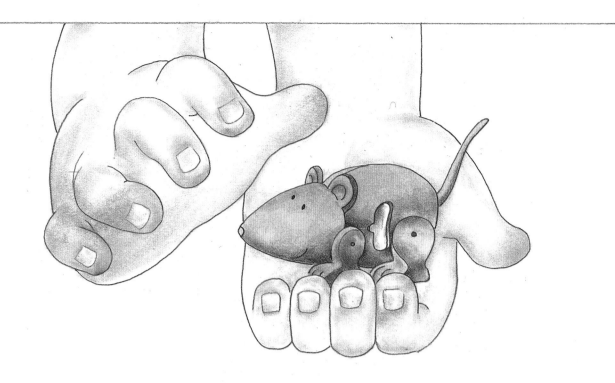

The other kids at school offered to trade their windup toys for Sputter. But Jasper would never do that, because Sputter was the fastest.

One day, Jasper received an early birthday present from his aunt! Inside was another toy mouse.

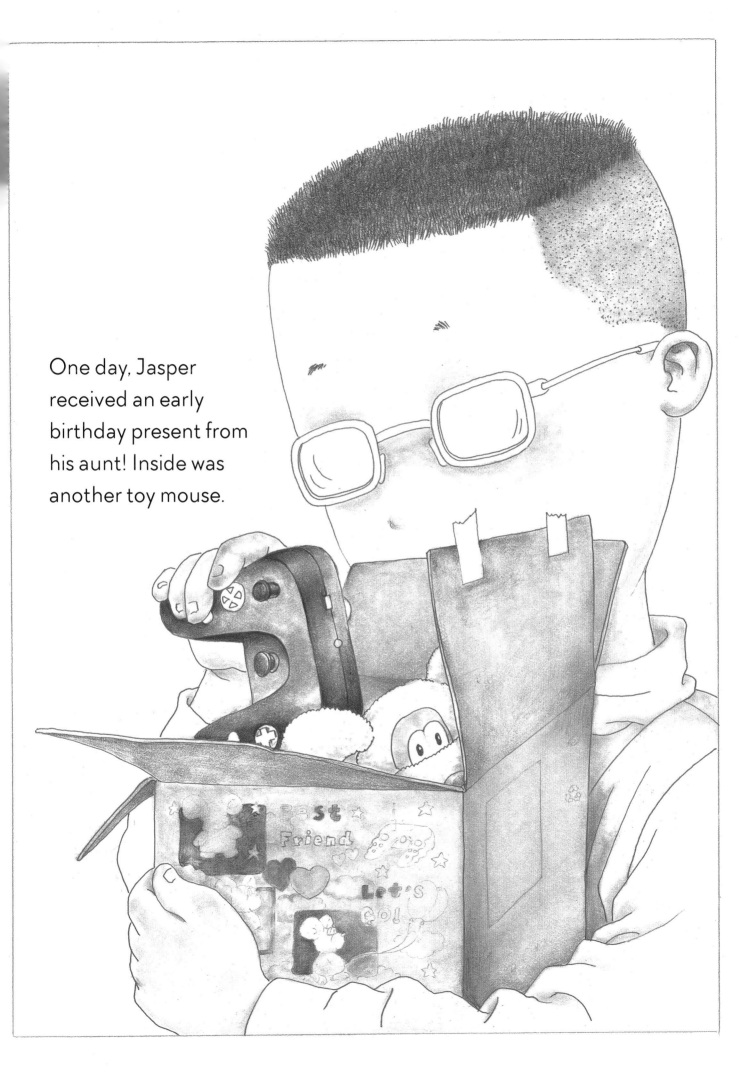

This mouse had a remote control, so Jasper called him RC.
RC could turn left or right, speed up or slow down, all from
Jasper using the remote control.

RC could zip and zoom even faster than Sputter. Jasper started to take him to the recess races instead of her.

But at home, Jasper would race RC and Sputter.
RC usually won, but Sputter was close behind.

After each race, RC told Sputter, "That was close!
You sure are fast."

Sputter replied, "I always zip a little quicker and
zoom a little farther when Jasper is cheering."

They became fast friends.

Months later, Jasper received a late birthday present from his uncle. Inside was another toy mouse. Jasper named it Charger.

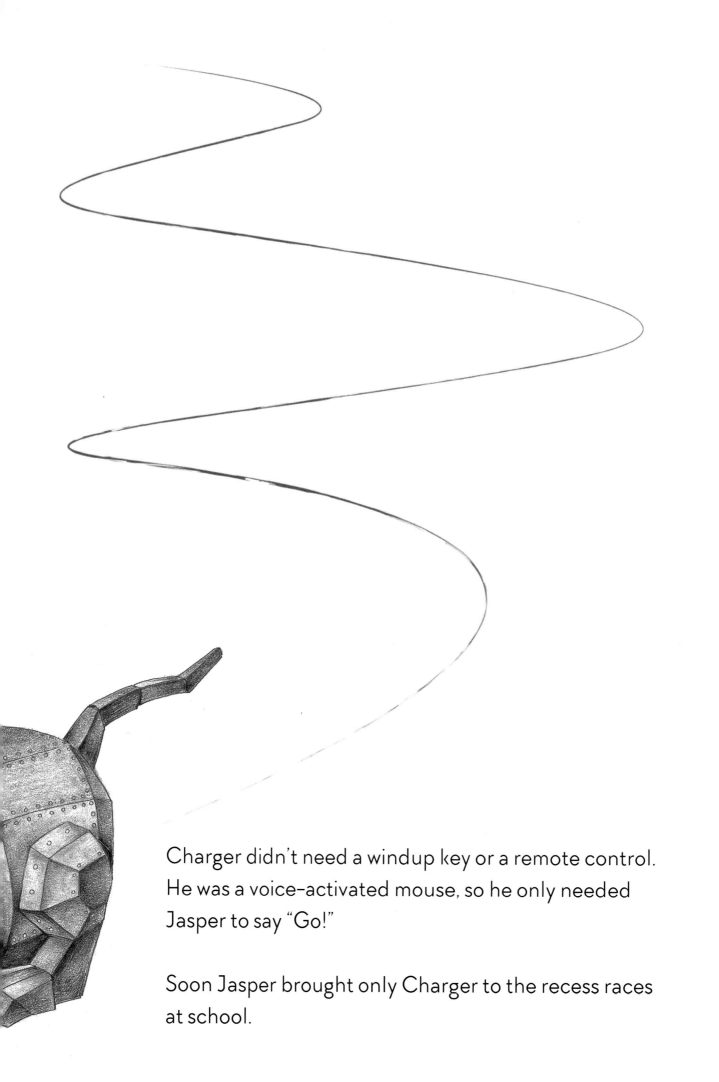

Charger didn't need a windup key or a remote control. He was a voice-activated mouse, so he only needed Jasper to say "Go!"

Soon Jasper brought only Charger to the recess races at school.

Charger did not want
Jasper to play with the
other toy mice. He told
the basement mice,
"If you get rid of those
toy mice, the boy might
want some pet mice instead."

The next morning, after Jasper left for school with Charger, the basement mice found RC. The mice circled around RC. Without his remote control, he couldn't go anywhere! They didn't notice Sputter nearby.

"We'll tear you apart and toss you in the trash!" yelled the basement mice. They pounced on RC and began to bite and scratch.

From her hiding place, Sputter could see everything. She was scared of the fierce basement mice. She wanted to save RC, but how could she possibly help? After all, she was just a windup mouse.

But RC was her best friend and he was in trouble!

She needed to stop acting like a windup chicken
and start acting like a windup mouse.

Then Sputter did something she had never done before. She reached back and turned her own key three times. Charge!

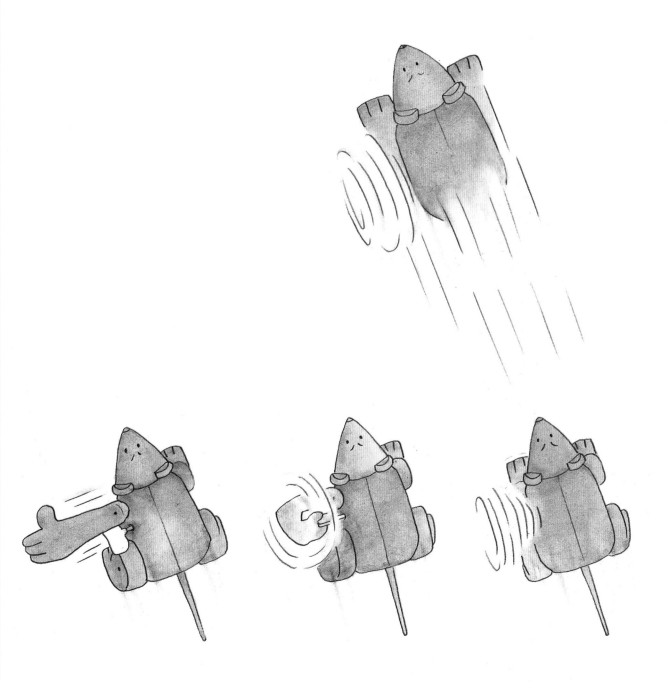

Click-clack click-clack click-clack!
Sputter imagined that Jasper was
cheering for her, which made her zip
a little quicker and zoom a little farther.

The mice turned to see what made
the noise. "Eek!" They squeaked
in fear and scattered. They
weren't so brave when a toy
mouse stood up to them!

When Jasper came home, he saw Sputter and RC
in the middle of the room. Had he left them there?
"I'm glad it's Charger I lost at recess and not you
two," said Jasper. "How about a little race?"

And the two fast friends did just that.

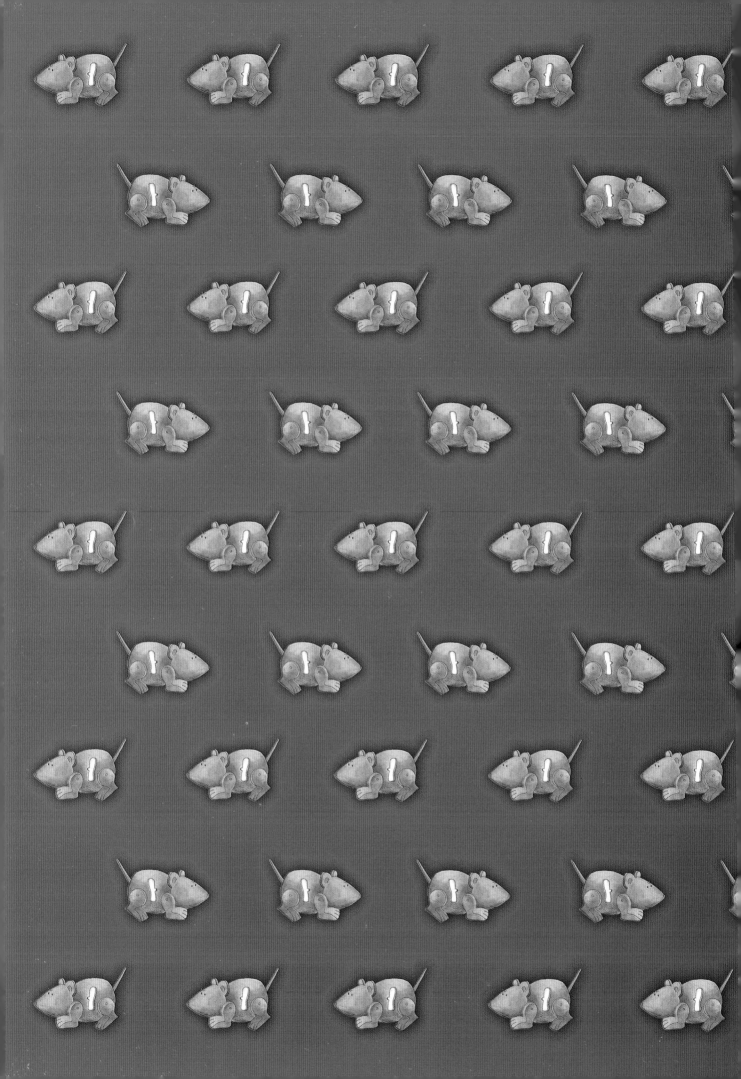